PUPPY PATROL ™

TUFF'S LUCK

TUFF'S LUCK

JENNY DALE

Illustrations by Mick Reid
Cover illustration by Michael Rowe

AN
APPLE
PAPERBACK

SCHOLASTIC INC.
New York Toronto London Auckland Sydney
Mexico City New Delhi Hong Kong Buenos Aires

ISBN 0-439-44935-9

Copyright © 1998 by Working Partners Limited.
Illustrations copyright © 1998 by Mick Reid.

All rights reserved. Published by Scholastic Inc., 557 Broadway, New York, NY 10012, by arrangement with Macmillan Children's Books, a division of Macmillan Publishers Ltd.

SCHOLASTIC and associated logos are trademarks and/or registered trademarks of Scholastic Inc.

12 11 10 9 8 7   6/0

Printed in the U.S.A.

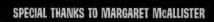

SPECIAL THANKS TO MARGARET McALLISTER

CHAPTER ONE

"**T**his is the best school trip ever," said Neil Parker, bending down to ruffle the ears of a Jack Russell terrier snuffling at his feet. "I never realized schoolwork could be so interesting!"

Neil's class from Meadowbank School had taken over Priorsfield Farm, near Compton, for a morning field trip in bright, spring sunshine. Neil picked up a short stick and held it in the air above his head. He watched as the little dog's tail wagged eagerly and his eyes lit up with anticipation. Neil hurled the stick across the farmyard toward two huge barns, and the terrier scampered off to retrieve it.

Chris Wilson and Hasheem Lindon, two of Neil's friends, stood nearby and grinned at each other. They knew what to expect from Neil Parker when it came to dogs.

"Typical," said Hasheem, chuckling. "If you took Neil to the North Pole, he'd find a dog."

Chris Wilson laughed. "If you took him to Mars he'd still find a dog!" Neil's family ran a boarding kennel just outside Compton and dogs were his life. "Hey, Neil!" Chris yelled. "Have you finished drawing that map yet? We could go and help bottle-feed one of the orphan lambs."

"Or go and see the new Jersey calf in the shed," said Hasheem. "It's a little wobbly on its legs and covered in goo, but you should go and see it."

"In a minute," said Neil, watching the terrier pounce on the stick with a growl, give it a good shake, and then bound back so that he could do it all over again. "Anyway, lambs and calves are fine, but look at this dog — he's the star around here!" He patted the dog's tan-and-white coat and tickled his stumpy ears.

Chris and Hasheem looked at each other again and shrugged. It was hopeless trying to get Neil to concentrate on anything else.

The farmer, Harry Grey, emerged from one of the outbuildings filled with yellow hay bales and came toward them. He was a tall, lean man with a weathered face. He pulled wisps of straw from his gray hair as he walked. His brown jacket looked as lived-

in as his face. He smiled at Neil and said, "That's Tuff."

"What's tough?" replied Neil, looking surprised. "Do we have to go now?"

"No, son. That's the dog's name: Tuff. He was such a scrap of a pup when he was born that we didn't expect him to live. But as you can see, he's a spirited little fella and he pulled through. He's been making his presence felt around here ever since!"

"I think he's great," Neil said eagerly. "How old is he?"

Before the farmer could reply, a woman in jeans came out of the house behind them and shouted

Tuff's name. Neil guessed that she must be the farmer's wife. Tuff ran to greet her and trotted at her heels as she came to join them.

"You've made friends with this little rascal, have you? He eats us out of house and home," she said, allowing the dog to tug playfully at the legs of her jeans. "None of our other dogs seem to eat as much as Tuff and some of them are three times his size!"

"True, but Tuff's a first-rate farm dog," said Harry Grey. "He's as good as any collie with the animals, and he keeps the vermin down, too."

"I bet he does. He's really agile, isn't he?" Neil threw the stick one more time and Tuff scampered off.

Mrs. Grey looked at Neil with approval. "I can see you're used to dogs."

Chris and Hasheem laughed.

Mr. and Mrs. Grey suddenly looked puzzled, wondering what was so funny.

"Neil's mom and dad run King Street Kennels," explained Hasheem. "It's a boarding kennel where they look after dogs whose owners are away. They've also got a rescue center where they take in abandoned dogs and strays and find homes for them."

"Really?" said Mr. Grey, nodding with interest. "It's handy to know where I might find a good working dog if I need one. Look out, kids, here comes your teacher."

Mr. Hamley joined the group, looking every inch a country gentleman in his sturdy boots, barn jacket, and peaked cap. "This is very kind of you, Harry, putting up with fifty eleven-year-olds swarming around your property." He eyed Neil and his friends suspiciously. "Neil Parker, have you finished your map of the farm as I asked you to?"

Neil's face colored slightly as he handed his teacher a half-completed sketch of the farm buildings and surrounding fields. He'd marked the positions of some of the fields and the woods, but not what they were used for, and he had completely left out the river.

"Mmmm," mumbled Mr. Hamley, scratching his chin. "Hardly a masterpiece, is it, Neil? Did something distract you by any chance? A dog, perhaps?"

"Well, sir," Neil said apologetically, "I only said a quick hello to Tuff. I . . ." He broke off as he looked around for the energetic Jack Russell terrier. "Where is Tuff, anyway?" asked Neil worriedly, as he scanned the nearest green field. The dog was nowhere in sight.

"Tuff? Who's Tuff?" asked Mr. Hamley, firmly.

"Tuff is Mr. Grey's Jack Russell. Wait, isn't that his bark?"

They all listened. There was a steady, urgent barking coming from somewhere beyond the farmyard.

"You're right," agreed the farmer. "That does sound like our Tuff. Something's up!" He strode off through a gate and into the nearest field. Neil didn't wait for permission from his teacher but fell into step behind the man, adopting the same purposeful stride.

The sound was coming from beyond a rough, bumpy meadow that sloped downhill toward the river. Something was making Tuff bark frantically and Neil could think of nothing else as he stumbled through the tall grass. Mr. Hamley, Chris, and Hasheem followed several yards behind him.

"There he is!" cried Neil, pointing to a dense hawthorn hedge on one side of the meadow. Tuff was running backward and forward in front of a narrow section of it, barking a canine alarm.

The farmer quickened his pace as he approached the point where Tuff was now waiting for them. "This time," he muttered to himself, "this time, there'll be trouble. I'll get him, whoever he is."

Neil was about to ask him what he meant, when another sound caught his attention as he pulled up in front of the hedge. He could hear the whimpering of an animal in pain.

"Don't touch anything!" There was a firm hand on Neil's arm as the farmer caught up with him. "Let me deal with this." Neil stood back as the man squatted down and peered under the hedge. "It's old Mick!"

Almost hidden under the hedge, a stumpy, rough-haired mongrel lay shuddering in discomfort and struggling to move. He was bigger and shaggier than Tuff and was desperately straining to remove something that gripped his leg tightly. Neil caught a glimpse of something glinting against the dog's shaggy coat.

Mr. Grey's face clouded over with anger and distress as he crouched down to survey the scene. "What's that on his leg?" asked Neil.

"It's a snare," replied the farmer, his voice shaking with emotion. He pushed back the dried grass to reveal the grisly contraption that was gripping his dog. "He's trapped. I knew something like this would happen. All right, Mick, take it easy." The farmer tried to soothe the distressed dog, stroking its rough coat. He turned to Neil. "I could really use some help here. Can you hold his head and keep him calm, while I try to loosen this wire? Be careful, though. He doesn't usually bite, but he's terrified, and you're a stranger to him."

Neil was glad to help. He knelt by Mick's head, holding him firmly and talking gently to him, while Mr. Grey carefully began to unwrap a brass wire from the dog's left hind leg. Tuff had calmed down but stayed close by, watching them at work. Neil could see that freeing Mick was a delicate job, which had to be done with great care to avoid causing the dog any more pain. The wire had cut into his leg quite badly, and his fur was stained with blood. Mr. Hamley, Chris, and Hasheem appeared behind them but didn't say anything. They watched intently as Mr. Grey concentrated on freeing the wounded dog.

"There you go, Mick. That's that," said Mr. Grey at last. He climbed to his feet and scowled, the gleaming wire in his hand. "Up you go, boy." The dog struggled to stand, but collapsed immediately and sat licking his sore leg.

"These things can be lethal," said Mr. Grey, as he held up the wire. The noose that had grasped Mick's leg was clearly visible at one end.

"Is that a snare?" asked Mr. Hamley, peering closely at the device.

"Yes, it's meant for rabbits," said Mr. Grey. "A rabbit runs along the hedge, catches his head in there, the noose pulls tight and then it's caught fast until the person who set it comes back to collect his dinner."

"That's awful," said Chris, in a hushed voice.

"Yes, it is. Unfortunately, it also means that any other animal that runs along here gets caught, too. It's a brutal, indiscriminate weapon. There's been a poacher up to no good in the woods for a while now, but he's never come this close to the farm buildings before."

Neil watched as Mick struggled to stand up again. "Who do you think it might be?"

"If I knew that," said the farmer, "he'd have had the police to answer to long before now. He's been causing appalling damage. I've had sheep getting their feet caught in these recently. The more an animal panics and struggles, the tighter the snare gets. Poor Mick has made a mess of his leg by doing the same thing."

Neil gently helped to pick the dog up and Mr. Grey carefully cradled Mick in his arms so that the injured leg was not rubbing against anything. The small group began their somber walk back to the farm.

"Poor old Mick," said Hasheem in a concerned voice. "Do you think he'll be OK?"

The farmer shook his head. "I really don't think he'll be the same again, I'm afraid. He's an old dog, and a bit slow. His working days were already nearly over. He won't be any use on the farm now — except maybe as a pet."

"It does look like a nasty injury," said Neil.

"He's been Tuff's partner for years," the farmer explained. "They've been a great team working with the stock, keeping the animals together and in order. They're fast and eager, and like to be busy. We use them to catch rats around the place, too."

"Yuck! Rats!" squirmed Hasheem.

The farmer managed a smile. "You're on a farm now, son. You can't afford to be squeamish around here. Rats are vermin. We don't want them in the feed store eating everything and spreading diseases, so we keep a pair of good, keen little dogs."

"Wow. So Tuff is a pretty hard worker then?" asked Chris.

"You could say that. It's normally Tuff who flushes them out from wherever they're hiding. He tunnels into the straw bales in the barns. Mick is usually waiting to catch them."

"Do the rats suffer?" asked Neil. He didn't like to think of any animal being hurt, even a rat.

"They don't know a thing about it," the farmer reassured him. "As soon as the dog pounces, the rat's dead."

"And now this poacher has forced your team apart," said Neil. "Poor Tuff. I hope he'll be OK without his best friend." He leaned down and gave Tuff a quick pat and a scratch under the chin.

"I thought it was only large, country estates that had trouble with poachers," said Mr. Hamley.

"This poacher doesn't seem that fussy," replied Mr. Grey. "There's so much woodland and wildlife around here, that it's just the right sort of place for him to thrive."

"You said he'd been causing damage, Mr. Grey. What sort of damage?" asked Neil.

"There's some woodland a bit further along the river that is a protected conservation area. Quite a few of the farmers around here have worked hard to make it a good environment for wildlife — it's got some great features. There's even an old icehouse in there somewhere."

Chris looked baffled and was about to ask what an icehouse was, but the farmer kept on talking.

"Well, he's been in there, too, this poacher, probably after pheasants," Mr. Grey continued. "He drops old shotgun cartridges all over the place."

"I was up near there earlier this morning with a class identifying different types of trees," said Mr. Hamley. "A lot of the new saplings have been crushed. Did he do that, too?"

"That's probably him. He doesn't seem to care what gets trampled when he goes blundering around in there. The fences and hedges don't seem to stop him either. We're always having to make repairs and I just can't afford to have my men dealing with this sort of thing all the time. We've got too much to do. It's costing us hundreds of dollars."

"And now this," said Neil sadly, looking at old Mick lying sedately in the farmer's arms.

"Yes, this is definitely the worst. I've never found a trap so close to the farm before. He's getting bolder as he tries to find more and more game in the woods."

They arrived back at the farm and Mr. Hamley

held open the gate, ushering them through. Mr. Grey didn't say another word, but headed straight for the house to call the local vet, Mike Turner. The teacher looked at Neil's worried face as his gaze followed the farmer until he had disappeared from view. "Come on, Neil. Don't worry. Mr. Grey will get Mick the best attention there is. I'll round up the others and meet you back at the bus."

Chris and Hasheem watched Mr. Hamley disappear among the farm buildings and then looked back at their friend. Neil was leaning against the gate, surveying the woods and the river beyond the field from where they'd just walked.

"Are you OK, Neil?" asked Chris.

"He's out there somewhere," Neil replied, his face tense with anger.

"Who is?"

"The poacher. The man who's been causing all this damage. The man who hurt Mick."

"But there's nothing we can do about it, Neil."

Neil's face hardened into a steely look that Chris had seen several times before. It meant Neil had made up his mind to do something. "Oh yes there is. He's got to be caught before he harms any more dogs. Before he hurts Tuff. And I'm going to catch him."

CHAPTER TWO

At King Street Kennels, it was feeding time for the dogs, and Carole Parker was busy measuring dry dog food into a row of dog dishes. Neil's mother, a very tall, dark-haired woman, kept glancing at a clipboard as she worked to check that each dog was given the right meal. It wasn't easy to concentrate with Neil talking nonstop in her right ear.

Neil had returned home from school excited about his visit to Priorsfield Farm and hadn't shut up about it since. His sister Emily was perched on a stool with her head bent over a book about dogs. She was two years younger than Neil but just as devoted to dogs and animal causes. Five-year-old Sarah was barely tall enough to reach the counter, but grabbed and carried dog bowls for her mother nevertheless.

"It's terrible that this man is allowed to keep on getting away with it," Neil was saying. "Something has got to be done. Mick was in a really bad way when we found him. Tuff could be next — and the injuries could be even worse!"

"Were there any hens?" asked Emily. "I like hens."

Neil thought for a moment. "Hens? Er, yes, I think so. Mr. Grey said we weren't supposed to feed them, but Chris dropped half a cheese sandwich and a pickle and I think they liked it. Hasheem said they'd all lay pickled eggs."

"I don't suppose it'll do them any harm," said Carole, without looking up from her list.

"But what have hens got to do with it? I was talking about Tuff and the problem Mr. Grey has with the poacher." Neil desperately wanted to interest his sister and mother in the terrible injustice he had discovered that morning.

"Poacher? Who's got a poacher?" Neil's father said as he entered the King Street storeroom and deposited a sack of woodchips beside the bench. He was a big man, with broad shoulders, who seemed to take up half the room just by standing there.

"Oh, Bob, there you are," said Carole. "You're just in time to help with the evening feed. Can you carry the bowls for the rescue dogs? Emily, will you do the water bowls?"

The whole family helped to feed the dogs — even little Sarah joined in, always trying hard not to trail her pigtails in the water or the food, and making a great fuss over all her favorite dogs.

Kate McGuire, the full-time kennel assistant, was just returning from walking four of the boarding dogs. A tall, slim figure in leggings and a baggy sweatshirt, with her long blonde hair tied back in a ponytail, she returned each pooch to its rightful pen. All the dogs loved Kate. She worked as hard as the Parkers to keep the kennels clean and comfortable, and to make sure the dogs felt welcome.

There was a great deal of barking and yapping and wagging of tails as feeding time began, and Neil and Emily helped distribute the different bowls. King Street had two kennel blocks, each with two rows of ten pens, and a central aisle. There were exercise runs, too, so that every dog had all the space that it needed to run around. Ten pens in a separate block were kept for "rescue dogs" — the strays and abandoned animals that were brought in to King Street from time to time. Neil didn't often get angry, but the sight of a neglected dog made him furious.

"Half of Compton must be on vacation this week — we're totally full right now," Kate said as she opened a pen and rubbed the ears of a little black crossbred collie. "Here you are, Cassie. There's a good girl. Neil, can you take the blue bowl in to Buttons? Jed and Sally and all the regulars are here — I never understand why everybody wants to go away at the same time."

After they'd finished feeding all the dogs and Bob had secured the kennels for the evening, Kate rode her bike home to her apartment in Compton.

The Parkers sat down together in the kitchen for their dinner. When everyone was seated around the big wooden table with large helpings of Bob Parker's mouth-watering spaghetti Bolognese, Neil started telling them about what had happened to Mick. "I was wondering if there was a rescue dog that would be suitable as Tuff's new ratting partner, Dad."

Bob Parker frowned thoughtfully. "The trouble with the rescue dogs is that very often they're too nervous to be working dogs. When they first come here they may have had a rough time with their owners, so they don't trust anyone and will be quite defensive. Or they may just be shy. Remember what Sam was like?"

Neil's own dog, Sam, was lying under the table with his head against Neil's foot. The black-and-white Border collie pricked up his ears and thumped his tail at the sound of his name. Sam had been a thin, hungry, and very frightened pup when he had first arrived at King Street five years earlier. Now he was a healthy, happy dog and Neil's devoted friend — he was even an expert at agility competitions — but it had taken time and patience to win his trust.

"It takes a long time to get a nervous dog to settle down," Bob went on. "Some of them never really do. At the moment, I don't think we've got anything

suitable. But, if you like, I'll have a chat with Harry Grey and see what he's looking for."

Sam nuzzled Neil's foot under the table.

"I know, Sam, you'd love to try ratting," said Neil. "But I can't spare you."

"No, he wouldn't, Neil! It sounds so cruel!" protested Emily. "Even if I do hate rats."

"Mr. Grey says it's not," said Neil. "You should see Tuff in action. All that happens is —"

"Thank you, Neil!" interrupted Carole Parker firmly. "We don't want to discuss ratting while we're at the table. Emily, what have you been doing at school? Have you got any homework?"

"I've been trying to tell you — if I could have gotten

a word in," said Emily, with a glance over at Neil. "I'm doing a project. We've all got to do an animal project, and I'm doing one about dogs."

"There's a surprise," said Bob, barely managing to keep a straight face.

"I'm doing a section on dogs with ESP," said Emily. "I've been reading all about it."

Carole laughed. "Don't they get an injection for that?"

"Mom," said Emily, "it means extrasensory perception. Sometimes dogs can sense things that humans don't know about. Some dogs can even tell when the weather's going to change."

"They can certainly tell when an owner is nervous or tense," said Bob. "You just have to sit in on an obedience class to see that." Bob ran sessions in their converted barn twice a week for owners with unruly pets. He'd probably taught half the dogs in Compton to sit on command, including Mr. Hamley's unruly Dalmatian, Dotty. "If the owner is uneasy, so is the dog. They can tell if you're scared of them, too."

"Fudge has ESP," said Sarah, matter-of-factly. Fudge was her hamster, and she was very proud of him. She still wasn't entirely sure what ESP was, but she thought Fudge ought to have it.

"There's lots of stories about it," said Emily, ignoring her sister. "My teacher says her little spaniel can tell when people can't be trusted. Sometimes ESP can be really creepy. Dogs won't go into a house that's haunted. They can sense that there's something spooky there."

"That's all we need," said Bob. "A kennel full of ghost-hunting mutts."

Neil laughed.

"You can laugh, Neil Parker, but strange things really do happen," insisted Emily. "Do you remember Mr. Andrews, that old Scottish man last year with the two Labradors? He used to say they wouldn't walk past the graveyard at night. There was a particular point where they used to stop and growl, their hair bristled and they wouldn't walk any further."

"Spooky!" said Neil sarcastically.

"Anyway, I'll call the farm tomorrow, Neil," said Bob. "I'll go over on Saturday to see exactly what Mr. Grey is looking for. I might be able to help at a later date. I suppose you'll want to come, too?"

"Of course," chuckled Neil.

"And me!" said Emily.

The King Street Kennels Range Rover drew up at the main gate of Priorsfield Farm on Saturday morning and parked on the grass. Neil and Emily, in old clothes and dirty sneakers, jumped out and ran to open the gate. To Neil's delight, the wiry, bright-eyed Jack Russell bounded to meet him, barking excitedly.

"Hi, Tuff! Remember me? Get out of the way, you jumpy thing, or you'll get run over. Heel! Good boy!"

Mr. Grey emerged from behind a rusty-looking tractor to see what Tuff was barking about. He smiled when he saw who had arrived and came to meet them. Mick, with his leg bandaged, limped slowly behind him.

"How's Mick?" Neil asked immediately.

"Not so bad," said the farmer. "He's had stitches in his leg and Mike Turner bandaged it up. He took good care of Mick and gave him something to ease the pain."

"Mike's our vet at the kennels, too," said Emily.

"Have you had any more trouble with the poacher?" asked Neil eagerly.

"Too much. I've just had to get all the sheep back into their field this morning. The poacher's been up to his tricks and this time he left a gate open. My sheep were on the main road and away up in the top meadow, too. It's taken me and the boys all morning to get them back in. Tuff did his bit to help, but he's been a bit quiet since Mick has been laid up. I think he's missing having another dog to work with."

Bob Parker held out his right hand to shake Mr. Grey's. "Morning, Harry. Good to see you again. Neil tells me you've got some trouble."

"Trouble is too kind a word, Bob. I don't know what I'd do to this guy if I ever found him."

"Have you spoken to the police?" asked Bob.

"Oh, yes, and I'm not the only one. All the farms around here have had problems, but the police have enough to do without standing watch here all night. They don't think it's serious enough yet to step up their efforts. It's just a series of isolated incidents to them, but to us it all adds up to one big problem."

Emily tugged on Neil's sleeve and pointed toward the door of the farmhouse. "Neil, there's another dog over there." A black-and-white collie was lying peacefully, curled up in a patch of sunlight on the porch, with a bowl of water beside her.

"That's old Cap," said Mr. Grey, noticing where they were looking. "She's a sweet old lady, that one. She's too old now to run around after the sheep, but she was a good sheepdog in her day."

"How old is she?" asked Neil, noticing the white hairs round the dog's muzzle.

"She's thirteen going on fourteen, I'd say, but she still enjoys life. She's got me worried, though."

"Cap!" Neil called, patting his legs. "Hello, Cap!" The dog stayed where she was, ignoring him.

"That's why I'm worried. She does that to me, sometimes, too," said Mr. Grey. "Doesn't always come when she's called. She's either getting a little grumpy in her old age or her hearing is beginning to go. I haven't had much time recently to confirm it either way — what with all this poaching business."

"I'll help, Mr. Grey. I might be able to find out what's wrong with her." Neil walked across the yard, crouched down in front of the old collie and tried calling her again. "Here, Cap!" She looked up and beat her tail against the ground. Then she rolled on to her back to have her tummy tickled. She seemed like a good-natured dog and was happy to make friends with him, nuzzling him and licking his hand if he stopped tickling her. "I wonder what your problem really is?" he whispered.

"Try something else with her, Neil," instructed Emily, coming to stand beside him.

"What's the matter with you? Cap, sit!" responded Neil.

The dog looked up at him adoringly as if she was wondering why he had stopped tickling her, and licked his hand. She was clearly not about to sit up on his command. Neil sat back on his heels, thinking hard. He looked at Emily for inspiration but she just shrugged her shoulders.

"Cap," he tried again, raising his arm to help her understand his command. "Sit!"

Cap gave him an inquiring look and stayed firmly sprawled on her back. Neil was certain an experienced sheepdog would be used to these commands.

Neil stood up and Cap, realizing that tummy-tickling was finished for the day, rolled over, sat up, and then looked at him. The dog cocked her head a little on one side. Neil was aware that she had only gotten up because she had wanted to, not because of his commands.

"Down," said Neil, pointing to the ground. At once Cap stretched out her forepaws and lay down. Neil

fussed over her and praised her, and she rolled over again. Perhaps he was making progress.

Emily clapped. "There! She did it that time!"

Encouraged, Neil continued his impromptu training session. "Sit!" he said confidently. His frustration returned when Cap ignored him again.

The collie began getting her teeth into a tangled patch of her coat.

"Neil, bend down in front of her and get her attention again — like Dad does in his obedience classes," suggested Emily.

Neil nodded and crouched down directly in the

dog's line of sight. "Cap, sit!" Seeing Neil raise his hand to his shoulder, Cap suddenly seemed to realize what was being asked of her, sat up at once, and fixed her intelligent black eyes on him.

"Good girl! Down!"

Neil pointed to the ground and the dog lay down. He began to scratch her under her chin.

"Do you think she's got ESP?" asked Emily. "Is she listening to things we can't hear?"

"Not this one," said Neil. "I don't think she can hear anything at all."

"What's that?" Harry Grey overheard Neil's remark and broke off his conversation with Bob Parker. "You think old Cap's a bit deaf, then?"

Neil was looking pleased with himself. "I think so. She does everything I say if I stand in front of her and use hand signals. It's only when she can't see a signal that she won't respond. She's not disobedient, she just can't hear what you tell her."

Mr. Grey stroked the old collie gently. "You may very well be right, son. Poor Cap. I was hoping it wouldn't be her hearing that had failed her."

"So what are you going to do with her, Harry?" said Bob Parker.

"Do with her?" repeated Neil, looking astonished. "You're not going to get rid of her, are you?"

CHAPTER THREE

"**W**e'll have to do something with her, Neil," repeated Bob Parker. "A deaf dog's not safe on a farm. Is it, Harry?"

Neil immediately clutched the collie tightly as if defending her from attack.

"That's right," confirmed Harry Grey. "There's tractors and cars and machinery coming and going. If she can't hear, she can't get out of the way. If I saw her running headlong into danger, she wouldn't hear me calling her back."

"Surely she's too old to go running off anywhere," said Emily.

"An old dog can still move fast," said Mr. Grey. "Especially if she thinks she's defending her territory."

"Has she always lived here, Harry?" asked Bob.

"She was born here. She's a wonderful dog. Her mother was the best sheepdog I ever had, and I trained Cap myself. I can't take any risks with her, especially now — I don't want another dog getting snared. A busy farm is not a safe place for a deaf dog, I'm afraid."

"But she wouldn't be happy anywhere else, would she, Mr. Grey?" pleaded Neil. "Not if she's lived here ever since she was a puppy."

Emily came to her brother's aid. "There must be something we can do, Dad. Would she be able to hear a dog whistle?"

Bob drew a shiny metal dog whistle from his pocket and blew hard. It had no effect on Cap. "She can't hear that one," he said. "But different whistles have different frequencies. I might have one at home that she could hear. She can certainly get by with hand signals, but that can only work when she's looking right at you."

Neil turned to the farmer, who was already grinning.

"I know what's coming next," said Mr. Grey. "You're going to ask me if you can both come back with a pocketful of whistles and try them all out on Cap. Well, I'd love to be able to keep her, so yes, I suppose so. Honestly, Bob, I've never seen a kid so crazy about dogs."

"Thanks, Mr. Grey," said Neil. "We'd love to try."

"Come tomorrow, if you like. Take her to the field —

the one where we found Mick — and see what you can do."

It was exactly what Neil had been hoping for. His return visit would be a great opportunity to do a bit of poacher hunting, too.

The next day, Neil and Chris Wilson arrived at Priorsfield Farm on their bikes, with Sam the Border collie running alongside them on the narrow country road. They pushed their bikes along the wide track that led toward the farm buildings and they chatted as the morning sun beat down on their backs.

"So why didn't Emily want to come? I thought you said she wanted to help Cap," said Chris.

Neil rolled his eyes. "She announced this morning that she had no intention of seeing Tuff or any other dog devour the local rodent population."

"Huh? I thought she was tougher than that. She virtually beat me up when I managed to get a goal past her at soccer practice last week!"

"She thinks it's immoral. Plus, she's scared of rats! With me it's spiders; with her it's rats."

As the two friends arrived at the farmyard they were met by Tuff who immediately wanted to make friends with Sam. The terrier barked at Sam's feet and ran around him several times before rushing off into the nearby field to run around some more.

Neil said a quick hello to Mr. and Mrs. Grey and

brought Cap away from her usual resting place on the farmhouse step.

"She's a great dog, Neil. I can see why you want to help her," Chris remarked as they entered the field.

"Look, Chris. Tuff thinks Sam's his new friend. I'm glad they've taken a shine to each other. We'd better get them on the leashes soon. I want to check the field."

"For what?"

"Snares. There might be some along the hedges or outside rabbit holes."

Chris struggled to hold on to the dogs' leashes as they tried to break free, while Neil walked around the periphery of the field checking for any of the poacher's deadly snares. Eventually Neil was satisfied that the ground was clear and came to Chris's rescue.

"You're not firm enough with them, Chris," he grinned. "Tuff! Sam! Sit!"

The dogs sat, and Chris relaxed.

"OK, now this is what I think we should do. You take them over there and let them play. Throw sticks for them. Just keep them active so Cap won't be looking at me. I'll blow the dog whistles and see if she responds to any of them."

When Chris was several yards away from him, Neil pulled a bunch of dog whistles from his backpack, of all different shapes and sizes. He isolated one from the bunch and blew hard into it. The sound was barely audible.

Neil kept his eyes on Cap, but the whistle sound brought no reaction at all. She went on chasing sticks and trying to keep up with the younger dogs. Sam and Tuff raised their heads at the sound, but Cap clearly couldn't hear anything. The second and third were no better, and the biggest of the bunch had no effect even though Neil blew into it until his cheeks turned pink.

After trying a long, thin, rusty whistle, which he suspected his dad had bought at least a hundred years ago, Neil let out a whoop of joy. All three dogs had raised their heads. Another blast from the ancient instrument brought Cap running to Neil's side, closely followed by Tuff and Sam.

"Well done, Cap! Well done!" There was no doubt

about it — Cap had definitely heard the sound and responded to it.

"That's the one," said Chris, coming back to join him. "She can certainly hear that."

Neil ruffled Cap's floppy ears. "We've figured Cap out — as long as her hearing doesn't get worse. Do you want to keep going and see if we can find any signs of a poacher by the river or the woods?"

"Do I have a choice?"

"No. C'mon. Bring Sam and Tuff. But keep a close eye on them once we clear the field. Don't let them stray off the paths — there might be some of the poacher's snares lying in wait."

"OK."

Sam, Tuff, and Cap soon ran ahead, scampering backward and forward with noses twitching at the ground and tails fanning the air. They climbed into another field bordering the river and continued upstream. Neil kept his eyes to the ground, in case a footprint or some evidence of poaching — a snare or spent cartridges — might give a clue to help him find out where the poacher had been.

"That's funny," he said as they approached a muddy patch on the riverbank. "What's the matter with Tuff?"

Where the spindly roots of a willow tree wove in and out of the ground, Tuff crouched, growling, his ears pricked, and his coat bristling. He barked a soft, uncertain bark, and backed away.

"Sam's doing it, too, look!" exclaimed Chris.

The black-and-white Border collie had stopped at the same spot and was retreating from it, growling softly, his head tipped to one side. Neil and Chris ran over to investigate.

"Is it another snare?" Chris said urgently.

Neil, too, had immediately suspected it was a snare but on closer inspection the brown earth seemed undisturbed apart from the usual amount of paw prints made by the woodland animals. But there was something there that the dogs found unfamiliar and puzzling.

"I can't understand it," said Neil. "But I think it's time we put them back on the leashes — just in case."

Cap sniffed the same spot with intense concentration. She gave a few short, warning barks, then she, too, backed away.

"You know what Emily would say, don't you?" said Neil, patting Cap as he clipped her leash into place. "She'd say it was . . ."

". . . Haunted!" whispered Chris.

"Or spooky!" added Neil. "The ghost of an old brown cow!"

"Or a vampire sheep!" said Chris.

"Or a were-rabbit! Come on. Let's get back. We can come back and have another look around one day after school this week."

The three dogs were first to arrive back at the farmyard gate, followed closely by Neil and Chris still giggling about ghosts and supernatural phenomena.

Neil was excited to tell Mr. Grey about his success with Cap and the whistle, but decided against it when he saw the farmer's expression. He was standing talking to one of his farm workers — in his hands he held a dead rabbit by its hind legs. Chris's face immediately showed he was disgusted.

Neil stuttered, "Was that . . . ?"

"Caught in a snare? Yes," said the farmer grimly. "If he has to set traps, he could at least bother to check them. It's true that rabbits are sometimes pests but that's no reason for this sort of thing. I found it in a snare in the reserve. It's been dead for goodness knows how long."

Chris was appalled. "The poor thing must have suffered terribly."

Neil knelt down and put his arms around Sam's neck, pressing his face against the dog's coat. If that had been Sam, or Tuff, or old Cap . . . He gazed up at the dead rabbit.

"I've a good mind to go out there at night and try and catch this vandal in the act," Mr. Grey said angrily.

"Do poachers always work at night?" asked Chris.

"Yes. They're all cowards, you see. They wouldn't dare show their faces while they're up to no good."

Neil stood up and told Mr. Grey his good news about Cap. The farmer didn't cheer up much so Neil hurriedly thanked him for letting them come again, and left the whistle with him. Neil grabbed Sam's leash and thrust Chris back to their bikes and down the lane away from the farm before his friend knew what was happening.

"Hey, what's the rush? Where are we going now in such a hurry?" Chris demanded.

"Wait till we get back to King Street. I've had an idea!"

Chris watched his friend speeding away from him and groaned.

CHAPTER FOUR

"**Y**ou want us to do *what*?" Chris stared at his friend in awe as he hung up Sam's leash on a hook on the kitchen door at King Street Kennels.

"You heard me." Neil's eyes shone with excitement. "I think it's a brilliant idea."

"You would. Camping out just for the fun of it — now that's a brilliant idea," Chris said defensively. "Staying up late, eating food in bed, reading by flashlight. . . . But going camping to stalk a poacher? That's not so smart is it? Danger, tension, the risk of bodily harm . . ."

"We wouldn't be *stalking* him, exactly," said Neil slyly. "We'd just be doing a bit of detective work to help catch him. We wouldn't have to talk to him or anything."

"You keep saying 'we,'" said Chris. "*We* aren't doing anything. *You* might be."

"Look at it like this, Chris. All we do is ask Mr. Grey if we can camp on his land overnight. We can go tonight if we work fast. We'll take Sam with us, and Tuff, too, if we're allowed. We can keep our eyes open for anything suspicious — someone creeping around late at night, that sort of thing. We'll take flashlights. If we see anything strange, we'll report it to Mr. Grey in the morning. We'll pretend we just happened to see it."

"What if the poacher sees us before we see him?"

"He's not going to do us any harm, is he? He'd probably just run for it. And we'll have at least one dog to protect us."

"If I don't go," said Chris, "I suppose you'll just go and do it anyway, on your own, won't you?"

"You bet," said Neil with a grin. Chris frowned a bit, but he gave in.

"OK, but how do we get the all-important parents to agree to this?"

"We're only asking if we can go camping," said Neil, and shrugged carelessly. "It's a holiday tomorrow, so they won't be worrying about school, and we've done it before. We don't need to say anything about the other business. Look, we're not going to do any harm, and we won't be in danger. Much." Neil looked at his friend. Chris was already biting his lip and looking worried. "Don't worry, Chris. We'll be alright."

To Neil's relief, everything went according to plan. With Mr. Grey's permission, the boys began to pitch their tent that evening in an empty field that was normally used for sheep. It was well out of sight of the farmhouse, and sloped down gently toward the river. Neil decided they should set up camp in the furthest corner by the water. As long as the daylight lasted, it would give them a good view of the farmland and the woods.

After the fourth attempt, the two boys managed to make their tent stay up and while Sam and Tuff, reunited for their forthcoming nighttime adventure, wore themselves out chasing rabbits they never had a chance of catching.

As the evening grew slightly cooler, Neil and Chris were happy to have the extra sweaters they had packed. They sat outside in the fading light and drank hot chocolate from a flask and devoured as many cookies in one evening as they would usually eat in a week.

The setting sun turned the sky pink, then gold, and fiery beyond the river.

"No sign of the poacher," said Neil, unable to hide his disappointment.

"Just as well, I say," replied Chris, after finishing his last chocolate cookie. "Let's go inside. We can

take a look around in the morning when it's light."
He turned and began to move around inside the
tent.

"It'll be too late then. Didn't you hear what Mr.
Grey said? Poachers operate at night."

From behind the tent flap Chris mumbled, "What
a shame."

Neil climbed inside and found a spot for his sleeping bag, lying down at an awkward angle to avoid
disturbing Tuff who was curled up, exhausted and
already asleep, in the middle.

"Where's Sam?" asked Chris sleepily.

"He's just outside. He'll stay out there and climb in
here later. He can be our guard dog!"

"I don't think we'll need one," moaned Chris.
"We've got no chance of getting any sleep. The
ground's way too bumpy. Ow! I think I'm lying on a
rock!"

"Stop whining. We had to be at this end of the field
so we could be near where the poacher struck last.
He might come back."

"Well, I'm going to try and get some sleep. Wake
me up if we're attacked in the middle of the night."
Chris turned over in his sleeping bag and closed his
eyes. "'Night."

Neil accepted defeat, gently stroked the sleeping
dog between them, and replied, "Good night." And
then whispered, "'Night, Sam."

*   *   *

Suddenly there was a noise.

Neil's eyes popped open and he sat up, still half inside his sleeping bag.

Tuff was growling a low, threatening rattle with his head turned toward the opening of the tent. Ears pricked, he stalked warily to the flap and poked his nose underneath.

Neil stared at the entrance to the tent. Outside, he heard Sam shuffle around and give a short, sharp bark.

Neil fumbled for the powerful flashlight he'd borrowed from his father, and switched it on. He shined it directly into Chris's face. "The poacher!" he whispered. "Wake up, Chris!"

Chris was immediately wide awake and shielded his eyes against the glare. "It might not be," he said, meekly. "It might just be Mr. Grey, checking up on us to see that we're OK."

"At this time of night?" Neil looked at his watch. "It's past midnight!" He crept forward and opened the tent flap a little, keeping one hand on Tuff's collar, while Chris put on his sweater and shoes.

Neil peered out into the darkness. Sam padded over toward him and nudged his hand with a wet nose, but Neil couldn't see anything. Both the dogs were sharply alert, giving low growls and restless barks.

"Shush, Sam! Tuff!" Neil strained to hear what the dogs had sensed.

There was a sound. A rustling noise that seemed to echo all around him. "Chris, what do you think? I'm sure I can hear something. I think it's coming from down by the river."

"It could be anything — a fox or something."

The thought of actually catching up with the poacher was too much for Neil. Pulling his head back into the tent, he hurriedly flung aside his sleeping bag and laced up his sneakers. "Where are the dogs' leashes? Quick!"

"I guess I'll have to come with you," said Chris, handing him the leashes.

"Follow me," said Neil, and he was gone.

Neil emerged from the tent into the still of the night. There was a half-moon that helped penetrate the blackness, and gave everything an eerie, silver shadow. He felt shivers of fear and excitement. With a flashlight in one hand and Sam's leash in the other, he crept forward as softly as he could. Chris padded close behind him, with Tuff and a second light.

Chris stopped for a moment. "You're right," he whispered. "I can hear something, too. What was that?"

"A bat, I think," said Neil. "At least, I hope that's all it was. Listen."

They stood still and flashed their beams out in front of them. They listened, inched forward into the darkness, and listened again.

"It's by the river," whispered Chris.

There was more rustling and the sound of twigs snapping.

"Something's moving over there," said Neil in a low voice. He sounded braver than he felt. Then Chris, with a sharp gasp, pointed to the river.

"What's that?"

Neil saw it, too. A ghostly glow hung over the river-bank. It began to move. Then it stopped, and moved again. A cold chill of fear spread down Neil's spine and along his arms. The light stopped again.

"Is that the spot where we were on Sunday?" asked Chris, nervously. "The dogs didn't like it. They knew something was there. It's where they . . ." Chris's voice trailed off, suddenly afraid of the implications of what he was suggesting.

Just now, neither one of them wanted to think about the possibility that this stretch of the riverbank was haunted.

Neil's adrenaline was on overdrive. He kept on walking toward the light, partly driven by his need to find out who was causing Mr. Grey and his animals so much trouble, and partly because Sam was straining on his leash, tugging him onward. Behind them, Tuff was pulling Chris along, too, and on any other occasion Neil would have burst out laughing to see the little Jack Russell terrier tugging along such a big person.

They crossed the river to the opposite bank, their shoes and socks getting drenched from the chilly water that flowed over the rocks and shallow riverbed. For a second they stood on the riverbank, in the soft mud.

Then the light vanished.

There was a terrible cry. Something between a snarl and a scream tore through the air, followed by the sound of an animal in pain.

And then silence.

For a second Neil and Chris stared at each other, paralyzed with terror. Then they were crashing back through the water, stumbling back up the hill, tripping over rocks and thistles. They ran wildly past the tent, the two excited dogs pulling ahead of them, and pounded up the hill toward the farmhouse and safety.

When they felt they had put enough distance between themselves and the unseen horror at the river bank that had made that bloodcurdling cry, Neil and Chris began to talk to each other again. They spoke in quick, nervous, exhausted sentences as they ran.

"It's this way!" gasped Neil, his voice hoarse from the effort of running.

"I don't care. Just keep going!"

"That noise."

"It saw us. What was it?"

Suddenly Chris tripped. He dropped his flashlight, which disappeared into the long grass and went out. He groped around helplessly for it, wondering if the creature in the dark was following them.

Neil flashed his light on Chris. "It doesn't matter. We'll come back for it! Come on!"

Chris got up and ran on, occasionally losing his stride catching his foot in a rabbit hole or tripping on a molehill. He followed Neil until they came to a fence.

In the distance a sheep bleated and they both jumped.

"The sheep are — um — that way," Neil faltered. "And the farmhouse is — oh, I don't know."

It was growing colder. They were completely lost. Neil put his arms around Tuff's neck.

"Tuff might know!" he said, frantically unclipping the dog's leash. "Tuff, find home — find the house — find your boss!"

The terrier scampered off into the night and Neil, Chris, and Sam ran desperately after him.

CHAPTER FIVE

Mrs. Grey padded through the rooms of the farmhouse in her bathrobe, switching on lights as she went. A frantic banging on the heavy oak front door disturbed the quiet of an otherwise peaceful Priorsfield Farm.

"Coming!" she shouted.

As she unlocked the door and pulled it open, the banging suddenly stopped and two scared faces looked up at her.

"What's up with you two?" she asked, looking anxiously from one white-faced, muddy figure to the other. "What happened? Have you seen a ghost?"

"Yes," said Chris, in a very small voice. "I think so."

"You'd better come on in," she said, moving aside to let them through. "Come on. Bring the dogs in, too."

"Thanks," mumbled Neil as he traipsed mud through the hall to the stone floor tiles of the Greys' rustic-looking kitchen.

Mr. Grey arrived a few moments later and switched on the tea kettle. He chuckled and said, "Looks like you've got the jitters pretty bad. Want to stay here tonight, rather than go back to the tent — which I assume you've abandoned?"

"Yes, please," they chorused gratefully.

"If I'd known you wanted to act like you were the farming FBI, I would never have allowed you to go in the first place." Bob Parker chewed his breakfast and shot Neil another disapproving look across the kitchen table.

Neil munched on his cereal and tried to avoid Emily's stare as she giggled her way through her own breakfast, reveling in watching Neil squirm under interrogation from their parents.

"What did you two think you were doing?" asked Carole Parker.

"We heard noises and just wanted to go and see what was happening," Neil said lamely.

"And what exactly do you think you saw?" persisted Bob.

"I told you, Dad. Just this light — kind of dim and eerie. It was right at the place where the dogs had sensed something before. It moved. It was so weird . . ."

Emily burst out laughing.

"Emily . . ." said Carole.

"I'm not going to say 'I told you so,'" said Emily, her mouth twitching with laughter. "But I did. I think I should put that story in my project. I wish I'd been there with a camera when you two got back to the farm!"

"It was really scary, actually," insisted Neil.

"You'll need to go back later today, then," said his mother. "You've left your tent and all your gear behind."

"It'll be alright. I don't mind going back in daylight — as long as I don't have to go back to that spot!"

"Are you sure you'll be alright, Neil?" asked Emily innocently. "I can come and hold your hand, if you like."

"That's enough now," said Bob. "Are either of you going to help around the kennel today or not?"

Neil took his opportunity to escape further torment and fled the kitchen.

Emily rushed after him. "Don't worry, Neil. I'm right behind you. I'll protect you . . ."

Early that evening Neil and Chris were back at the farm, rolling up sleeping bags, collecting their various belongings, and packing away their tent. Sam and Tuff weren't much help. Tuff thought sleeping bags were for making tunnels and Sam thought he was playing hide-and-seek. In the daylight, the terrors of the night before seemed ridiculous. Neil still thought he'd never live it down, especially if Emily went on teasing him.

"Anyone would have been scared," said Chris. "It was spooky, because it was so dark and everything."

"Yes. And we still don't know what really happened." Neil sat down on his rolled-up bedding and pushed his hands through his spiky brown hair so that it stuck out more than ever. "We know what we saw. There was a light moving near the riverbank, about where that willow tree is. And we heard a yell. We didn't imagine that."

"There must be an explanation," said Chris. "I think it's a simple, normal one, with nothing spooky about it at all."

"And we're going to find out what it is," said Neil, brightening up. "Let's finish up here, stack it all up near the gate, and go and have a really good look down there. If it wasn't a ghost, who else would be hanging around in the middle of the night? This is the closest we've come to tracking down our poacher."

"Are you sure you want to go back there?" asked Chris.

"Positive," Neil replied adamantly.

Before they reached the riverbank, Neil clipped leashes onto the dogs' collars. "We can't let them go bounding in and disturbing any evidence. If we're going to do this, we should do it right. Chris, look — what do you think of that?"

On the far side of the riverbank the grass had been trampled and lay flat. The sandy mud closest to the river was marked with large, overlapping footprints.

"Must have been a very heavy ghost," said Neil.

"With big boots on," added Chris. They leaned closer to take a good look at the pattern left by the footprints. They could make out a crisscross design, and there were zigzags on the heel. "So much for the spooky light. A poacher with a flashlight, more likely. I wonder if . . . Hey, Neil!" He dropped his voice to a whisper. "What's that, moving by the river? No, not up there — under the roots of that tree!"

The boys crouched down, holding the dogs close and still. Sam and Tuff shuffled restlessly as if they had sensed something again. Their attention was concentrated on the spot beneath the willow tree where they had been spooked. As Neil and Chris watched in silence, a small black nose and whiskers appeared from a hole in the bank concealed by the willow's roots. The nose withdrew, and then appeared again. A brown, whiskery face peered out — a round, intelligent little face, bright-eyed and alert. The animal emerged gradually, a long, low, brown body easing itself down the bank — then with a graceful swoop it curved into the water, where it twisted, turned, and glided noiselessly.

"Oh, wow!" Chris whispered.

"An otter!" Neil exclaimed. "I've never seen one before! Isn't he beautiful!"

"He's a she," said Chris. "Look."

Another, smaller, face peeped from the hole in the riverbank, then another. The otter swam back, put her nose up to the hole in the bank, and nuzzled at the young, inquisitive face of an otter cub. Now there were three little faces pushing their way forward. Coaxing, nuzzling, and nudging them, the mother otter led her small, plump, clumsy little cubs slithering down the bank to the water. The first two sniffed at it, half-stepping and half-falling in, and bobbed

about precariously, rising to the surface to shake their whiskers and scrabble at the water with their paws. Their mother was never far away, swimming underneath them on her back; never leaving them in any danger as they learned to find their balance in the water. Then she returned to the timid cub mewing on the bank, nudging and leading it until it too was wriggling around in the water.

"They're fantastic!" said Neil, in a whisper. "Emily would go gaga if she was here. I bet Mr. Grey doesn't know about this. We'll have to tell him."

"Better be careful who else we tell, though," said Chris. "We don't want everybody coming down here and disturbing them."

"Better retreat with the dogs, too," said Neil. "They knew there was something here yesterday, so it's lucky they didn't find anything."

"I don't think Tuff would know the difference between a baby otter and a rat," added Chris.

"It makes it all the more important that we stop the poacher," Neil muttered.

Chris was horrified. "He wouldn't try to trap the otters, would he? They're a protected endangered species."

"Possibly," said Neil. "But he's bound to disturb them when he comes crashing around here. We've heard how careless he is. And what if he's left any snares lying around? Come on, let's get back to the farmhouse and report this."

"We should explore more of the river first," said Chris. "There might be more poacher clues. I'm starting to enjoy this."

"OK. You're on!" replied Neil. "He must have crossed the water, though. Look, there are footprints on the other side leading up across the meadow. The poacher might have fallen in. It could explain that scream."

They let the dogs off their leashes in the woods further upstream, knowing that they were at a safe distance from the otters. Neil and Chris kept watching where Sam and Tuff were wandering — making sure they didn't stray from the forest paths in case there might be any snares hidden in the undergrowth. When they had crossed over the river, getting their feet wet again, and after the dogs had shaken themselves dry and showered Neil and Chris from head to toe, the hunt for footprints began again in earnest.

Chris was the first to find what might be a clue. He knelt down to examine something made out of green nylon. "It's a net. Like a bit of old fishing net or something."

"There must be a rabbit warren around here," said Neil. Looking up, he saw that the rising ground was peppered with holes. "Mr. Grey told me about that. Poachers put a net across all the rabbit holes like these ones, and then send a dog in, so the rabbits run out and get caught in the net."

Chris grabbed Neil's arm. "Hey, where's Tuff gone?" he asked.

Sam was still sniffing at the net, but Tuff had vanished.

Neil's first thought was that Tuff had gone to try out his tunneling skills in the warren, but then he heard Tuff's sharp, urgent barking away to their left.

"Come on, Chris!" They ran off in pursuit with Sam at their heels. "What's he found this time?"

Tuff stood in front of a thick and tangled bramble patch. He was barking and growling with great excitement, making little jumps at it. He certainly would have worked his way inside it, if the vicious thorns hadn't pricked him.

"What is it, Tuff?" panted Chris.

"He's found something!" said Neil.

A padded blue glove, torn at the palm, had been caught on the brambles. Tuff was tugging at it with his teeth, fighting an imaginary battle with the bush until he ripped the glove away from the thorns.

"Give, Tuff," ordered Neil. "Good boy. This must be —"

"Shh! Listen!" said Chris. "Quiet, Tuff."

From deep inside the brambles came a low, thin whimper. In the heart of the thorn bushes, someone or something was in distress. Neil had already launched himself into the brambles, shielding his face with his arms, stepping on the branches, putting on the old glove to protect one hand. The whining cry of fear urged him on. Chris followed in the path Neil had made. Neil kept up his best animal-calming voice, though the thorns snagged on his clothes and scratched his legs.

"It's all right now, we're — ow! — we're coming. We won't hurt you. It's all — ouch — all right now. Easy, now. Ow! Ow! Gently. We'll get you out real soon."

Chris came up behind his shoulder, and together they looked down at a small black-and-tan dog caught among some roots and thorns. He looked exhausted, and had given up the struggle to free himself. There was blood on his coat and on the branches.

"Poor thing!" said Chris.

"It may not be as bad as it looks," said Neil. "He came in here looking for something, got caught, panicked, and has been thoroughly scratched and torn trying to get out. He's even got himself more tangled, too. The best thing would be to cut the twigs away, to set him free. Have you got your penknife?"

Chris nodded and reached into his back pocket.

"I'll hold on to him. You try and get him free."

"Do you think this is the poacher's dog?"

"Must be." The dog's deep brown eyes looked helplessly into his, and he felt fiercely angry as he cradled the matted dark head. "How can anyone do this to a dog? Easy, boy, keep still. How could he let him get caught like this, and just go off and leave him here?"

"I suppose the poacher tried to free him," said Chris, while he hacked at the twigs and binding branches of the bush. "That must be how he lost his glove. Think how dark it was. He probably couldn't get through to him because of his size. Maybe it was this little dog screaming last night. In pain! The poacher might come back to get him, you know. He could be out here now, looking for his dog!"

"Calm down, Chris! He won't come back. He doesn't care," muttered Neil. "Good dog. Keep still, now. You're almost free."

"Done!" called Chris, with satisfaction. "Good boy, you're free now." He reached out to stroke the frightened animal. There was a snarl, a snap, and Chris clutched at his right hand. "Ouch! What did you do that for?"

"Let me see!" said Neil. "Has he drawn blood?"

"Yes, a bit," said Chris through gritted teeth. He nursed his bitten hand. "I don't think it's very deep, but it stings."

"It was only because he was scared," Neil said defensively. "He doesn't know you. He didn't know you were trying to help. He only wanted to protect himself."

"Trust you to feel sorry for the dog. Now what do we do with him, anyway?"

"He's got a collar," said Neil, looking closely at it, "but no ID tag." He took Sam's leash from his pocket. "Now, boy, can you walk, or will you have to be carried? What's the matter with your paw?"

"Neil," said Chris softly, "I think I just heard something. Like something rustling around, on the other side of the hedge. Let's not hang out here, OK?"

Neil listened. Now that the dog had stopped whimpering, he could hear it, too. A rustle. A pause. A footstep. A sniff, and the sound of a cracking twig. There was a whiff of cigarette smoke. Tuff twitched and tensed his body. Sam growled a warning.

"Let's split, Neil. Now!"

"Just a minute," said Neil. While Chris impatiently stamped his foot, Neil stroked the dog's head and smoothly ran his hands down to his injured paw. Carefully, Neil drew a small thorn out from one of the dog's pads. He could see that the area was too badly hurt to walk on so he took off his jacket, already snagged and torn from the brambles, and wrapped the dog in it. Then he carried him out from the bramble patch.

"OK, let's go!"

CHAPTER SIX

Neil sat in the Parker kitchen alone, eating his dinner like a half-starved wolfhound. Emily had eaten much earlier with the rest of the family, but stayed at the table to keep him company with her head bent over her school project. Books and pictures were spread out across the table. Carole Parker watched Neil as the last, large helping of pasta disappeared and he pushed the empty plate to one side.

"So now we have one injured dog, one bitten hand, a family of otters, and a distressed jacket," she observed. "On the whole, it sounds like a fairly average day to me."

"Thanks for saving dinner for me," Neil responded sheepishly.

"You might like to know I just got off the phone with Chris's mom."

"Oh," said Neil as he gulped down a mouthful of tea. "Did she take him to the vet — I mean, the hospital?"

"The hospital, yes," said Carole. "Neil, try and remember which of your friends are dogs and which aren't."

"Count the legs, if it helps," suggested Emily, without looking up.

"Chris," Carole went on, "had his hand dressed and cleaned, and they gave him a tetanus shot. He didn't need stitches, though — it wasn't that bad. I wish you'd called home, Neil. You know how dangerous a trapped animal can be."

"Sorry. It was an emergency. I just wanted to get him out of there as fast as I could. Bramble was so upset."

"Bramble?"

"Bramble, the dog. We chose that name for him when we were carrying him back to the farm. It sounded right, because he was caught in the brambles. What's happened to him? He's alright, isn't he?"

"Your father took him to Mike Turner. He's checked him over and all of his vaccinations have been done, and he's had some first aid for cuts."

"So he'll be alright?" asked Neil hopefully.

"He needed a thorough washing, too. His coat wasn't in very good condition at all. He's staying at the animal hospital overnight for observations, but he should be back here tomorrow."

"Here?" Neil's face lit up.

"Yes, we'll keep him here as a rescue dog."

Bob came home at that moment, brushing dog hairs from his shirt.

"Hi, Dad!" Neil greeted him. "Will the dog be OK?"

"I think so, and so will Chris," said Bob. "I'm surprised his mother lets him anywhere near you."

Neil was about to protest, then decided he'd better not. A safer question might be in order. "What do you think of Bramble — the new dog?" he asked.

"I'll see how he behaves when he's settled down," said Bob. "We need to know if he's always aggressive. I can't let anyone have him until I know what his temperament is like, and whether he's likely to bite again."

"Do you think he's the poacher's dog?" asked Neil.

"It looks like it to me, and Mike Turner thinks so, too. He's dark, so he's easily hidden in the shadows, and virtually invisible at night. He's lean, so he'll be fast when he gets back to his old self again. He's small enough to go down a rabbit hole, and he's long in the body. Did you notice that? It makes him a good dog for tunneling and creeping around in the undergrowth."

"Will you tell the police about him?"

"I tell the police about every rescue dog, in case

they're reported missing. But I'll be surprised if anyone claims him."

"Yes," agreed Carole. "Claiming Bramble would be
as good as admitting to poaching, and I don't think
even your hopeless poacher at Priorsfield Farm would
be as dense as that."

"You took a big risk when you rescued him, Neil,"
said Bob. "What were you and Chris doing over
there, that far up the river? It's nowhere near where
you camped."

"We were just taking Tuff and Sam for a long
walk," explained Neil. He knew that sounded a bit
lame, but it was the best he could come up with. "We
were never off the farm land."

"Why are you so keen . . ." began Bob — but he
was interrupted by a cry from upstairs.

"That'll be Sarah wanting her bedtime story," said
Carole. "Could you, Bob?"

As Bob Parker left the kitchen, he turned around
and directed his parting remark at Neil. "We'll talk
tomorrow," he said ominously, and Neil gulped.

Neil and Emily arrived home from school on Thursday
afternoon and both immediately noticed a strange
car parked in the front driveway of King Street Kennels. The shabby state of the vehicle caught Neil's attention most. It was very old — a dark red color, with
battered paintwork, rusty wheels, several cracked
windows, and no sideview mirrors. It looked as if

something was about to drop off, but you couldn't be sure what.

"What a heap!" said Emily. "It's a wonder it still runs."

"I've never seen that one before," said Neil. He saw his dad and waved as he wheeled his bike to the garage. "Hi, Dad! Whose is . . ." Neil stopped short when he caught sight of the man at his father's side — probably the car's owner. "Oh . . . um . . . hello."

Bob raised his eyebrows at Neil.

The visitor was tall and thin. He appeared to be in his late twenties, but Neil couldn't be sure because his face was stubbly and dirty. His jeans and checked shirt were faded and his straggly brown hair looked in dire need of a shampoo. The man fidgeted nervously as he talked to Bob, and Neil wondered what he was doing here.

Neil decided not to interrupt them further and went through to the rescue center to look in on Bramble.

The dog was sleeping in his pen. Neil crouched down and peered through the wire mesh. Bramble looked very calm — hardly the dangerous dog that he was supposed to be at all. Neil looked up when he heard his father's voice.

Through the mesh on the door he could see the two figures walking toward him. The visitor never looked directly at Bob as he talked — he glanced from side to side and looked around him, as if he was searching for something.

"Yes, I realize that you want to choose a rescue dog for a pet," Neil heard his father say, "but I'm afraid that wanting a pet isn't really enough. At King Street, we care about the welfare of all our dogs, and we need to know that every dog is going to a suitable owner."

"I thought you'd be glad to get rid of them," grunted the man. "You get plenty of stray dogs, don't you?"

"That's not the way we look at things," said Bob. He was very calm and polite, but Neil knew he was annoyed. "Most of these dogs have already had bad experiences. We don't want to send them to another one."

"Had any new dogs brought in this week?" asked the man suddenly. "Say, in the last few days?"

They entered the rescue center and the man regarded Neil sullenly.

"Have you ever had a dog before?" Bob asked him.

"Oh, yeah, I've had lots of them. I want a black one this time."

Again, Bob changed the subject.

"Tell me about the dogs you've had before, pedigrees or mongrels?"

"Oh, er . . . both. Look, I only came to choose a dog. I want a small one."

"Dogs need a lot of exercise. Would you be able to provide that? And what about feeding — what have you fed your dogs on in the past?"

The man looked up and saw Bramble in the pen beside Neil. For a moment, he didn't say anything.

He just stared straight ahead at the sleeping dog in his basket.

"Feeding, Mr. Smith? You were going to tell me what you used to feed your previous pets?" pressed Bob.

The man's behavior suddenly took another strange turn. He muttered something angrily about the time, turned around abruptly without saying thank you or good-bye, and left.

Neil and his father stared at each other in disbelief.

From in front of the house they heard the rattle of a noisy engine, the roar of a broken-down exhaust pipe, followed by a cacophony of howling from the dogs in the kennel who wanted to join in with the noisy chorus.

"Well done, Dad!" Neil exclaimed. "I didn't like the look of him at all."

"Neither did I," said Bob suspiciously. "I didn't believe a word he said, and he certainly wasn't getting one of our dogs. He just wanted to get a rescue dog and get out, as fast as possible — no questions asked. And not just any old rescue dog, either."

"What do you mean?" asked Neil.

"He mentioned a small dog. A black one. In other words, a dog like Bramble." Bob looked down at Bramble and then seemed to read Neil's thoughts as he gave his father an astonished look. "Don't worry, I wasn't going to let him near Bramble."

Neil sighed. "He looks a little better today. His scratches are healing."

Bramble seemed in far better condition than the

matted, torn dog they had freed from the thorn bushes. His dark, thick coat, freshly washed and brushed, was soft and smooth. He stirred and took a couple of steps around his pen. When Neil tried to coax him forward to the wire mesh for a snack, the dog retreated and growled softly.

"He's still a bit shy, Dad, but I don't think he's likely to bite again."

"Let's wait and see, shall we?" Bob opened the door of the pen. The dog backed away and barked. "He looks like a little street fighter to me."

"That's just because he's been badly handled," said Neil. "Maybe he's a bit insecure. But he's bright. Aren't you, Bramble?" Neil tried again with a small biscuit and held it out toward him. The dog approached him warily, but this time without growling. His stumpy tail wagged as he accepted the biscuit.

Footsteps sounded on the gravel outside the center and Bob looked up. He waved at the man approaching them and indicated for him to come through. Mike Turner, the vet, visited King Street Kennels twice a week and whenever Bob had any emergencies. Today, Bramble was first on his list of patients to see. He needed to check that his cuts and scratches were healing, and inspect his coat.

"Hi, Bob, Neil. How's he's holding up?" asked Mike, cheerily, putting his bag down. "He doesn't know how lucky he is, this one, having Neil's tender loving care on tap twenty-four hours a day," he teased.

"I hope we find him a better home than his last one," said Neil. "Something better than being a poacher's dog."

Mike frowned while he examined Bramble. "The funny thing is that I've had someone asking about him already. Or about a dog like him. A man turned up at the animal hospital today asking if a black, shaggy little mongrel had been brought in. Sounds as though he was after this one, if you ask me."

"What did he look like?" asked Neil urgently. "We've had somebody fishy asking questions, too. Was he tall and thin, with long, greasy hair?"

"Nothing like it," Mike chuckled. "He was pretty

short and stocky. In fact he didn't have much hair at all. It was Janice, my nurse, who saw him, actually. And she didn't like the look of him."

"Did she say anything to him?" pressed Neil.

Mike checked Bramble's gums and teeth. The animal seemed to respond to the vet's expert and firm touch. "No, she wouldn't tell him a thing. She said she couldn't give information about any animal we had treated unless she knew she was talking to the owner. He got really nasty after that, and threatened to force his way to look for himself. Janice calmly picked up the phone and said she was calling the police. He called her a few names but then left in a big hurry. I didn't quite know what to make of it all."

"Well," said Bob, "all this interest in Bramble. He's the most popular dog on the block. Where do you suppose all this is leading?"

"I don't think we need to worry," said Mike. "Neither of them got what they wanted. Maybe it's a case of disputed ownership and they can't agree who the dog belongs to. And if they think we'll involve the police if they try anything unsavory, I don't think we'll hear from either of them again."

Neil looked at Bramble and hoped he was right. His mind was racing with possibilities about who these strange men were. He was convinced one of them would turn out to be Mr. Grey's problematic poacher.

CHAPTER SEVEN

Neil planned to spend as much time as possible at Priorsfield Farm that weekend. Helping to catch the poacher was a priority. He had persuaded Chris to skip soccer practice on Saturday morning and ride up to see Tuff and Mr. Grey. As they approached the gate, they saw a police car pulling away from the farm.

Neil and Chris exchanged anxious glances.

Farmer Grey emerged from one of the feed sheds and waved the two boys through. A rattle of noisy barks announced that Tuff wasn't far behind him, and the Jack Russell terrier bounded into sight and greeted them enthusiastically.

Mr. Grey, however, looked serious. "We've just had the police over. He's at it again."

"Oh, no," gasped Neil.

"What's happened now?" asked Chris.

"We think two of our lambs have been stolen. Right from under our noses in the near field." The farmer kicked the hard earth in frustration. "He cut through the barbed wire and just left it hanging — Tuff nearly got his ear torn on it."

"That's awful," said Neil, stroking the farmer's little terrier. He was genuinely fearful for Tuff's safety now that the poacher had dared to strike so close.

"There's a tarp missing, too," added Mr. Grey. "And a spade I left out last night. I think he's just helping himself to whatever he wants. I can't believe he thinks he can get away with it!"

"Can we do anything to help?" asked Neil.

"I don't think so, but thanks for offering. If you could give Tuff a long walk this morning that would take a weight off my mind, though. I think he's missing running around with old Mick. Remember to shut the gates behind you, that's all."

"Of course we will," said Neil, mustering a smile despite the grave situation.

Mr. Grey looked around absent-mindedly. "Now, where did I leave my hammer? I'll need to get the repairs started on that fence." He looked at the little Jack Russell, whose ears had pricked up. "Tuff! Fetch the hammer!"

Tuff turned and scurried around the yard, sniffing and poking his snout into holes and under bushes. Miraculously, he soon found Mr. Grey's hammer with its distinctive blue handle beside a gatepost and clamped his mouth around it. It looked heavy as he carried it back, hanging lopsidedly from his jaws, but he soon laid it proudly at the farmer's feet.

"That's amazing!" said Neil. "Does he really know what a hammer is?"

The farmer managed to laugh, too. "No! If I'd called for the pliers or my pair of wire-cutters — I've lost them, too — he would have brought the hammer! He just seems to like carrying it. Well done, Tuff."

Neil picked up the hammer and handed it to the farmer. "See you later," said Neil as they turned and headed off for their walk. "We'll have him back before lunchtime."

Tuff was in a playful mood as they crossed the fields. Chris threw a stick for him and the dog scurried off, scrambling through the long grass and hedges until he returned, proudly holding the stick clamped between his jaws. A gray clump of earth suddenly came to life and a rabbit raced across the field to the safety of a hole in the ground. Tuff raced after it enthusiastically, but the animal was too fast for him.

They crossed the river at the same point they had done several days earlier and had another thorough soaking when Tuff, sneezing and shaking, shook himself dry after a cool morning dip.

"What exactly are we looking for this time?" asked Chris, after a while.

"Tracks, I suppose," said Neil. "We're pretty certain the poacher has been in this area, because we found Bramble and the glove not far from here. And there was the net. And remember the pattern of his boots, from the footprints by the river? That crisscross and zigzag pattern, we'll have to look out for that. It's a shame we have gravel on all the paths at King Street — we might have been able to identify the poacher when he came to snoop around."

"*If* it was the poacher, Neil. It might not have been him."

"I'm sure it was. You didn't see him, Chris. He was really shady — even Dad thought so. He must live somewhere around here. Maybe we can find his hideout. We could search for clues like the police do, scouring every inch of the ground."

"But they do it in long lines with plenty of officers," Chris pointed out. "And there's only two of us."

They searched as thoroughly as they could, but it wasn't encouraging. Away from the edges of the water there was no soft earth to show footprints, and no mud. The ground around the thicket where they found Bramble was well worn down, though.

"It looks as if he tried to get the dog out," said Neil. "I hope so. Maybe he really did care about him. But I've got a feeling he doesn't understand dogs, just like he doesn't understand the countryside. Let's go deeper into the woods — try some of the trails. He must have used some of them to get around and he may have left tracks."

Several rough footpaths stretched through the woodland on both sides, and Neil and Chris followed the widest path leading away from the river. After twenty minutes of fairly rough terrain they seated themselves on a fallen tree and shared a can of lemonade.

"We've drawn a blank," said Neil. "I don't know where we go from here."

"We're not going to catch any poachers this way, Neil," said Chris. "Let's go back to the farm — Tuff's probably already had the longest walk of his life. We could see how Mick is. And how Cap's getting along with the whistle."

Neil thought for a moment and was then struck by an idea. "Chris, when we were camping, what did we hear?"

"Rustling — moving about," replied Chris, wondering where Neil was going with this. "And then that noise."

"Exactly. But what didn't we hear?"

"A brass band and a fireworks display?"

"No. An engine noise. It would be pretty difficult to get a car anywhere near here anyway. It's too bumpy and too narrow."

"What are you getting at?"

"If he didn't have wheels, he might live fairly close by. And there aren't many houses around here, are there? And he wouldn't want to trek for miles and miles every day to get here. Come on, Chris. Let's follow the paths leading away from the farm and see where they lead to. Any houses within reasonable walking distance are a possibility."

"So we're walking further, then?" asked Chris, rubbing his feet and pretending they were already sore.

Neil looked at his watch. "OK, maybe not this morning. We did say we'd get back for lunch. But first thing tomorrow, yes?"

Chris was up and already walking back the way

they had come. Tuff ran after him. "Tomorrow it is . . ."

That night, Neil was in a deep sleep and dreaming. Tuff was chasing rabbits that turned into wire-cutters as soon as he caught them. Then Tuff some-how turned into an otter, and didn't like being an otter, so he threw back his head and howled. He turned into a wolf and brayed at the moon. The noise echoed around Neil's brain and wouldn't stop.

Neil woke up with a jolt. He shook his head but the howling went on. And then he heard a bell ring-ing. He shook his head again but it didn't stop. It was real. He reached over to the bedside table to put on the light and find his watch — it was ten after two in the morning.

From outside he could hear an alarm and the sound of several dogs barking. He scrambled across to his window and looked outside. All the lights around the kennel and courtyard were on and light-ing up the night sky.

He bumped into Emily as he rushed out of his bed-room.

"Neil! What's happening? I can hear Mom and Dad downstairs," she said urgently.

"I don't know! Come on!" Neil jumped down the stairs two at a time in his haste to find out.

Sam was in the kitchen, barking furiously at the back door, which was closed. Emily held him back and tried to calm him down. Neil's mother was on the phone. She held her hand over the mouthpiece for a moment while she spoke. "Someone's gotten into the kennel. Your father is out there now. I'm calling the police."

"Are the dogs alright?" asked Neil.

Bob Parker suddenly burst in through the back door and slammed it shut behind him. He was wrapped up in a thick jacket on top of his pajamas. He looked around at the three anxious faces — each desperate for news of what was going on. "They're gone — whoever it was, they're gone."

"What were they looking for?" whispered Emily.

Bob Parker sighed. "They were only after one thing, and it's the worst possible news. I'm afraid they've stolen a dog."

"Which . . . dog?" Neil asked hesitantly. He almost knew what his father was going to say before he answered.

"It's Bramble, Neil. He's gone."

CHAPTER EIGHT

"I'm really not happy about your going up there again, Neil," said Carole Parker the next morning. Neil sat glumly on a swivel chair as his mother took advantage of the rare peace and quiet of early Sunday morning to catch up on some office administration. "What do you think, Bob?"

Bob Parker shuffled through files and folders nearby, looking for insurance forms and security system details. The break-in had really shaken him, and he'd decided to cancel the morning's obedience class.

"What is all this about, Neil? Why are you so set on going out there again?"

Neil shifted uncomfortably on his seat. "Chris and

I want to go to the farm for the day, that's all. To walk the dogs."

Bob raised an eyebrow. "Isn't Mr. Grey getting tired of you two turning up?"

"Not yet. He says it's good for Tuff. And we can help him out a bit with the other animals."

"It isn't just that," said Carole, turning away from the screen. "It's all this poaching business. I think you and Chris are getting too involved in something that could turn out to be dangerous."

"Up to now," said Bob, "we thought this was just some clueless guy blundering around the country-side. But whoever stole Bramble last night was de-termined to get what he wanted."

"I'm worried about Bramble," said Neil. "I couldn't get back to sleep, thinking about him."

"I know," said Bob. "I don't think any of us slept much last night. But remember, whoever came for Bramble last night was desperate. That's why you can't get too involved."

"It must have been that man with the old battered car," said Neil. "The one who came last week."

"Maybe, but we can't be sure," said Bob. "It's all in the hands of the police now, and I've given them a de-scription of the man I thought I saw last night."

Carole Parker sighed and gave in. "Neil, you can go on the condition that if you spot *anything* suspi-cious, you head straight back to the farmhouse and tell Mr. Grey about it. *Don't* take any stupid risks. And Neil, be careful."

"Of course I will. I never go looking for trouble!" Neil protested.

"I know, I know. You just seem to find it."

Neil and Chris arrived at the farm later that morning and immediately dug into their packed lunches. Sitting on a fallen tree in the field by the farmhouse, they ate their sandwiches and watched Tuff and Sam play in the grass.

"So are we going to look for the poacher?" asked Chris, nibbling a carrot. "Even after the warnings your parents gave you?"

Neil swallowed his mouthful of food. " 'Course we are. And Dad only told me to be careful out here. He didn't exactly tell me not to go looking for the poacher."

"But did you tell him that's what you intended to do?"

"Not exactly."

Chris shook his head and mumbled, "Why am I friends with you, Neil?"

Neil gathered his things and shoved them into his backpack. "Because it's exciting. Let's go."

Chris smiled and dug around in his various pockets looking for Tuff's leash, discovering a few old tissues, candy wrappers, and a pack of chewing gum he'd forgotten about. Then he stopped. "Neil! Look what I found." He pulled out a glove from his inside pocket, and Neil recognized it at once. It was the glove they had found in the bushes when they rescued Bramble.

"We should have handed that in to the police, I suppose," said Chris. "I'd forgotten all about it."

"So had I," said Neil. "We were so busy looking after Bramble that we forgot about everything else. Hey, what are you doing?"

Chris was showing the glove to Tuff, who sniffed it and seemed to think he was being offered a new toy. He tugged it hard, growling, and when Chris finally let go, gave it a thorough shaking.

"I think it's dead now, Tuff," said Neil. Chris was watching the dog keenly.

"I want him to pick up the scent," he said. "If he can get the poacher's scent from the glove, he'll be able to lead us to him."

"No chance!" said Neil. "Only specially trained tracker dogs can do that. Besides, that glove's been stuffed in your pocket for a week. It might smell of toffee or mints. At the very least, it'll smell of you — and you shouldn't inflict that on any dog. It won't have any of the poacher's scent left on it after all this time."

"I'm going to try anyway," said Chris determinedly. When they reached the woods, Chris held the glove near Tuff's wet nose again and encouraged him to try and track the scent. "Come on, Tuff! Find the poacher!"

Neil smiled, but followed them along one of the footpaths with Sam anyway. Every couple of minutes, when Tuff had wandered off the path or stopped to investigate a boring-looking tree stump, Chris would stop to show the glove to the terrier again. Tuff kept dropping it, hoping that somebody would throw it for him to chase.

The footpaths eventually emerged onto some wider minor roads that criss-crossed through the trees and all over the farmland. Tuff seemed to show no sign of stopping so Chris urged them on.

When they reached the few houses along one road bordering the trees it was midafternoon, and they took a good look at each building as they passed. There were two with very expensive cars outside, elegantly draped curtains at the windows, and large, well-kept gardens — one even had a goldfish pond.

"I don't think so," said Neil, catching the hopeful look on Chris's face.

"OK, I must admit, the people who live here probably wouldn't bother with poaching," said Chris.

Further down the road there was another row of cottages, set further back into the woods.

"Let's try those. I think we've come too far, though. I bet the poacher would have a shack rather than a

normal house." Neil looked up the road as he held
Sam tightly by his leash in case there were any pass-
ing cars.

"You might be right, but we may as well go back
that way," said Chris. "There'll probably be another
path back through the woods when we get past the
cottages."

Chris was right. As they reached the end of the
row, they saw a marker leading to a path into the
trees across a small clearing. They let the dogs off
their leashes and were about to begin their long
walk home when Tuff's familiar warning bark dis-
tracted them.

He had bounded ahead and was barking in front of
a large tarp-covered object. Half-screened by the low
hanging branches of several trees, the shape resem-
bled a car or a small van.

Neil and Chris looked at each other.

"What do you think?" said Neil, excitedly.

"Definitely looks strange," said Chris. "It's a bit
too far out of the way to belong to one of the cottages."

"Keep a lookout," instructed Neil. "And keep an
eye on Sam and I'll go and see."

Chris stayed by the marker and surveyed the surrounding area. Neil looked around and moved toward
Tuff and the large object. He ducked in front of it,
quieted Tuff down, and then lifted one corner of
the heavy gray tarp. As Neil looked over at Chris,

about to shout out what it was, he registered his friend's frantic waving of his arms. Someone was coming.

Neil dropped the cover, gathered Tuff into his arms, and rushed back to Chris.

"We've got to hide!" said Chris, urgently. "I can hear noises in the trees. Look, over there! There's something coming toward us. It might be him!"

The steady sounds of boots and crackling of leaves as someone trudged through the woods was clearly audible.

"Over there! Behind those bushes!" Neil immediately shoved his friend toward a dense bundle of low leaves and branches. They crouched down behind them, Neil kept Tuff quiet and Chris desperately tried to soothe Sam by stroking his head and saying "ssh" in his ear.

"It's that car!" whispered Neil urgently. "I'd know that rust bucket anywhere! It's the one we saw at King Street! The man who came looking for Bramble, that's his car!"

Chris's eyes met Neil's. They stared at each other incredulously.

Suddenly an unfamiliar figure emerged from the woodland path and stopped. He was short and stocky, with a tough all-terrain jacket and khakis. He looked over the fence toward the covered shape as if checking that it was still there.

Neil felt Chris tense up and looked at him.

Silently Chris gestured to Neil to look down toward the ground where the man was standing.

There was a shape. A black dog. It was Bramble.

"He's got Bramble!" whispered Chris.

"But he's not the man who came to King Street," said Neil. "Who is he?"

"Didn't Mike Turner say he'd had a funny-looking visitor, too? A fat guy who turned up at the animal hospital asking about Bramble. That must be him! At least Bramble looks alright; he hasn't been harmed."

The man seemed satisfied that the car was undisturbed and moved out of sight, walking along the fence. He was soon hidden by the trees and the slope of the ground. Straining to listen, Neil and Chris heard the retreating footsteps, which crunched through the dry undergrowth come to a halt. Then there was a rattle and a creak.

"Back to the farm, as fast as we can," urged Chris.

"Wait! That sounded like a door opening," said Neil. "There must be a shed or something through there. It could be his hideout."

"I didn't see one," said Chris. "It must be well hidden."

They heard the door sound again, the man emerged from the trees, picked one of the footpaths, and walked away into the trees toward the river. Bramble followed him.

"We should try to locate his hideout," said Neil. "We can report it to Mr. Grey and the police."

"But he might come back any minute, Neil. It's too risky."

They broke cover and hurried down over the small hill, making as little noise as possible.

"No sign of a shed," said Chris, looking around. "But we both definitely heard a door."

Neil stopped, his eyes wide with surprise. "What's that?" He pointed to a rectangular shape, outlined on the sloping earth by uneven moss and a variation in color.

"It looks like a door in the hill!" Chris exclaimed. "Weird!"

Brushing away the loose moss, Neil revealed an old wooden door with a lock that seemed to lead directly into the hillside. Then Neil suddenly recalled something from their first visit to the farm.

"The icehouse! I remember now! Mr. Grey said there was an abandoned one in the woods! He's using it as a hideout!" Already Neil was trying the door and rattling the rusty lock.

"Hold on. I'm not going in there. It'll be freezing! These things are used for storing ice, aren't they?"

"Ages ago, maybe. But this one will have been left alone for years, I bet. It'll just be very cold. Honest."

Chris didn't look as if he entirely believed his friend's explanation but he helped Neil's efforts at getting the door open anyway. To their surprise, the lock gave way with minimum resistance and fell away as the door swung open. For a moment they stood at the entrance saying nothing, looking into the gloom and at the secrets it concealed.

After a moment's hesitation, they both stepped forward into the darkness. Light streaming in from the doorway behind them revealed that the roof was dome-shaped inside and lined with bricks. There was a camping stove, a pile of blankets, and two sleeping bags. Cigarette butts were everywhere and the acrid smell of nicotine wafted out. Dirty coffee mugs, stained dishes with twisted knives and forks, and crumpled newspapers littered the floor. More ominously, there were clear signs that this was a poacher's lair, as well as someone's home.

"There's your evidence, anyway," said Chris.

Neil took a single step further into the poacher's underground hideout. He turned his head away from two dead rabbits and a pheasant that hung upside down from a hook on the wall. A shotgun was propped in a corner. A camouflage jacket was slumped on the back of a chair, along with a net like the one they had found near the river, and a roll of brass wire. Tuff scuttled through into the icehouse before Neil could stop him.

"Tuff! Come back!"

The dog sniffed around the floor with interest and they saw him pick something up with his teeth. He climbed over the debris on the floor and emerged with a pair of wire-cutters in his mouth. Neil rescued them from his jaws and was about to throw them back inside when he noticed some writing on the blue grips. The name GREY was written on one handle in black marker.

Chris reached inside and picked up an old envelope that was lying at his feet. A map was sketched on the back. "Look familiar?" he asked.

Neil studied it closely. "It's a map of our kennel!" The thought that the poacher had taken such a calculated interest in King Street was scary. "Look, there's the rescue block. Come on. I've seen enough.

I think there are *two* poachers here and this situation has just become twice as dangerous. What's the quickest way back to Priorsfield Farm?"

"By following that man. We can skirt around him and get ahead by using some of the other paths near the river."

As they turned to make a run for it, Sam and Tuff were already bounding ahead, out of the icehouse and into the woods.

As Neil caught up with the two dogs he realized that their path was blocked by a tall, lanky figure. With a growing sense of horror, Neil recognized him. The man in front of them was the one who had come looking for Bramble at King Street Kennels. It was one of the poachers and he'd caught them both red-handed.

CHAPTER NINE

The wiry poacher stood menacingly in front of Neil and Chris and blocked their escape route. He stared at them, his eyes filled with silent threats. Looking over Neil's shoulder he caught sight of the open door to his secret den.

Suddenly his face exploded in anger, and he lunged forward and tried to grab at Neil. Tuff reacted first and went at the man's ankles, momentarily making him lose his balance — giving Neil and Chris the opportunity to start running.

There was no time to be afraid. Without stopping to think, they ducked one way, dodged the other, and tore through the woods with the poacher behind them. They could hear the swish and crackle of the undergrowth as he pounded after them, and Neil, gasping

for breath, expected to feel a strong hand grab at his arm at any moment. Sam and Tuff caught up to them and raced ahead, both enjoying the excitement of running though the trees at such speed.

"Left!" panted Chris, and the boys swerved — then behind them came a crash, a curse, and a scuffle. The poacher had fallen. They stumbled to a halt, and turned around.

The poacher lay sprawled on the grass, rolling on his back, muttering to himself and cursing. With both hands, he clutched at his right leg.

"It's a trick," gasped Chris. Still watching him, breathless, they stood shoulder to shoulder.

"Just a minute," said Neil, inching forward. He was straining to get a closer look.

"Don't," whispered Chris. "He's just waiting for you to get near enough, then he'll grab you."

"If he does, run for the farm," said Neil.

The man, still clutching his leg, seemed to be in real pain, but Neil didn't want to get too close, just in case. Peering from a distance, he caught sight of a familiar gleam of brass wire. The poacher made a clumsy attempt to try and clamber to his feet, but he fell down again with a cry and pulled off his boot and sock.

By this time, Neil could see all he needed to see. The poacher's foot had become thoroughly tangled and twisted in the running wire of one of his own snares. His awkward, heavy fall meant that the ankle caught in the wire was already bruised and beginning to swell.

"Run for the farm anyway, Chris. Get help," Neil said urgently. "I'll stand guard."

"I can't leave you," protested Chris. "What if he gets up and goes after you?"

"I'll keep the dogs with me. Just run."

Chris ran, and, as Neil called their names, Tuff and Sam bounded through the bushes to his side.

The poacher, sitting up, rubbed at his leg with both hands, and glared at Neil.

"You think you're really clever, don't you?" he muttered. His teeth were clenched and he continued to glower at Neil. On the ground he didn't seem fierce or dangerous. Seeing him nursing his foot and seething with helpless anger, Neil almost felt sorry for him.

"Just you wait till my brother gets here," he said, scowling as he rubbed at his leg. "You'll wish you hadn't been so nosy."

"Your brother?" Neil remembered the man he had seen at the icehouse, and Mike Turner's story of the man at the animal hospital, asking about Bramble.

The man's mouth twisted into a half-smile, half-scowl.

"You never caught him, did you?" the man sneered. "That guy at the kennel chased him, but he never caught him. None of the farmers ever caught him, either. Just wait until Carl comes."

Neil looked around, wondering where Carl might be, hoping he was miles away, deep in the woods. "I'm not sure you two could find your way out of a paper bag. Do you have any idea of the damage you've both done around here?"

"Carl knows all about these woods. He knows all about animals. He's good with animals, especially dogs."

"Good with animals?" Neil was too angry to be cautious. "Do you call poaching 'good with animals'? You didn't see the farm dog trapped in the snare. Have you ever seen animals struggling to get free from those things? And what about your dog? The one you abandoned in the brambles? We had to rescue him!"

"Carl tried to get Jack out, but he hurt his arm," grunted the man. "What did you go and take him for?"

The man tried to stand but he fell again and crumpled into a heap, clutching his injured leg.

"Tuff! Sam! On guard!" said Neil. He wasn't sure if Tuff would understand the command, but the dog's instincts and intelligence didn't fail him. Growling, both animals took their places at either side of Neil and tensed as if preparing to strike.

To Neil's surprise, the poacher's eyes widened with terror. He shuffled backward across the ground as much as he could, and his voice changed to a whimper. "Get your dogs off! Keep them off me!"

"They won't touch you," said Neil, "but you'd better stay put." Neil knew that Sam and Tuff would never attack a human being but they were clever enough to sense that the situation was tricky. This man had previously acted in a very threatening manner and they weren't letting their guard down for a moment.

As he stood facing the poacher, Neil thought about how long it would take Chris to get the farmer. They'd walked a fair distance from the farm, and Neil knew it wouldn't be long before Carl came looking for his brother. What was he supposed to do until then?

The poacher collected himself and stared at Neil again. "It's not as if old Grey even wants the rotten rabbits. They're a pest. They eat crops. We're doing him a favor. Carl says farmers want to get rid of rabbits."

"Sometimes they do," said Neil. "But not the way you do it."

"Never did any harm."

"You trampled his crops, too!" Neil pointed out.

"They'll grow again, won't they?"

"And you stole lambs."

"Did he notice? He's got so many, I didn't think he'd miss a couple. We had to have something to sell."

Neil couldn't believe what he was hearing. He almost laughed in amazement. "And you damaged his fences."

"Just a little bit!"

Neil gave up trying to reason with the man and chewed his lip with anger, afraid he might say something a lot worse than he already had.

A thin smile returned to the man's face. He was looking at something directly behind Neil. Then Neil heard a twig snap and an unpleasant, lingering silence. Whatever the poacher was grinning at, Neil might as well turn and face it. He heard a gruff, unpleasant voice.

"Having trouble, Gary?"

Trying to stay calm, Neil turned to see the man they had first seen at the road marker. Carl. At his feet was the familiar shape of Bramble — or Jack, as he was known by the two poachers.

By his side, Neil heard growling and instinctively knew that Sam and Tuff were ready to come to his defense. Carl had noticed them, too.

"Keep those dogs quiet," he ordered, and Neil decided it was safest to do as he said.

"Quiet, Sam. Quiet, Tuff. Easy. Lie down," Neil instructed them and they both did as they were told.

A stale smell of cigarette smoke wafted under Neil's nose, and he recognized the smell that had lingered in the icehouse. He knew for sure that he was in the presence of the men who had been guilty of endangering animals' lives. Knowing this fact hardened his resolve to not let them get the better of him.

"Now, do exactly as I say, kid, and nobody will get hurt," said Carl. "Gary, what happened to you?"

"Caught my foot in a wire," muttered Gary. "I can't walk."

"You can, with a little help," said Carl. The kid can give us a hand." He pulled Gary to his feet despite his brother's yelps of pain. "Come on, you," he said to Neil. "Hold on to him on the other side."

Neil would have liked to make a run for it, but he decided against it. With Carl and Neil holding on to Gary on either side, they walked the short distance back to the icehouse.

"It's all real nice for people like you," grumbled Carl, as they went through the wood. "You don't have to worry about where the money's coming from. We do. There's no harm in making a bit of extra cash out of a few rabbits. And there's good money to be made from pheasants and lambs."

"You don't have to do *this*!" protested Neil.

"Shut up, or you'll regret it." Finally, they reached the icehouse. Letting go of Gary, Carl took a firm hold of Neil's arm with one hand, and pushed Neil inside their makeshift home. Sam and Tuff ran in after him. Before Neil could make a dash for it, the door was slammed shut behind him and something was pulled across it to prevent him opening it.

"Prop yourself up against the door," he heard Carl

say, "and stay there." In the gloom inside the ice-house, Neil heard a creak from the door and assumed Gary had indeed taken up his post.

Neil shivered as he looked around the icehouse. There were no windows, only a tiny grille for ventilation in the roof, which offered very little light, and just one door. He continued to hear voices outside and pressed his ear up against the door to try and make out what was being said.

"He had a friend with him," Gary was saying. "I found them here, poking their noses in. His friend ran off. I bet he's gone to the farm to get help."

"Why didn't you say so before?" Carl said. "We've got to get out of here."

Locked in the icehouse, Neil felt a chill of fear spread through his body. Carl's next words filled him with a sense of doom and regret. His parents had been right — these people really were dangerous.

"The kid can stay in there and rot."

CHAPTER TEN

Neil looked around his icehouse prison and tried to figure out what he was going to do next. Sam and Tuff sat calmly by his feet. The wooden door was the only way in and the only way out. Neil thumped on the door. "Hey! Let me out! Let me out!"

The door swung open and light poured in.

"Shut it, kid. Keep screaming and you won't see your next birthday." Carl's face was twisted and ugly with anger. His plans had been shattered and he was having to think fast. He ignored Neil for a second and spoke to his brother again. "The sooner we're out of here, the better. Young Sherlock here has seen to that. We're finished if we stay. I could have used one more day — just one more so that I could get the otters."

"The otters!" said Neil, remembering the ghostly light on the riverbank. Even Gary looked surprised.

"Shut up, you!" said Carl. "Otters are worth a fortune if you know the right person to sell them to."

So, if the poaching had gone on for one more night, the otter family would have ended up as pets in somebody's backyard or as part of a fur coat. Whatever happened now, Neil was glad he'd prevented that. He kept his eyes on Carl, realizing there might still be a chance to escape, or, at least, to let one of the dogs out. Carl was in a hurry to leave, and he would certainly need more than one trip to take his poaching gear and the rest of their possessions to the car. He'd have to come back and help Gary, too.

Neil stroked Sam's head gently and together they inched forward into the open doorway and the daylight again. More than ever, he was grateful for all Sam's agility training. Sam would need it if Neil was going to stand a chance of escape.

"What about him?" Gary jerked his head in Neil's direction, and Carl glanced toward him.

"He can stay here," Carl said. "His friend will know where to find him. If you're worried about him, we can call the kennel when we're well out of the way, and tell them where he is." He shoved past Neil and roughly threw some of his belongings into a bag and slung it over his shoulder. He picked up an armful of nets, the rabbits, and a spade. "I'll put these in the car. Watch the kid until I get back — surely you can manage that, right? I'll be back in a minute."

"Sure thing, Carl. I'll watch him."

As soon as Carl was a few feet away, Neil let out a howl and surprised the younger brother who was supposed to be guarding him. "Go, Sam! Find Chris! Get him back here quickly," cried Neil, and Sam leapt out of the icehouse before Gary even knew what was happening.

The poacher looked up to see the light, graceful swerve of the Border collie as he sped away, and let out a stream of furious curses as Sam raced through the woods.

"Yes!" shouted Neil.

Carl's face shook with anger as he turned back toward Neil. He dropped his bag, the rabbits, and the nets, but kept hold of the spade and lifted it up menacingly in both hands.

"Carl . . ." croaked Gary nervously, but his brother wasn't listening.

"You little runt," Carl growled, advancing toward Neil. Neil wanted to run for cover, but the need to protect Tuff kept him rooted to the spot. Carl grunted and raised the spade above his head, and Neil took a small step back. "I've just about had enough of you . . ."

He didn't finish. There was a rising snarl and a snap as Tuff sprang forward, and a cry from Carl as the dog's teeth fastened into the sleeve of his jacket.

A violent shaking from Tuff loosened the man's grip and sent the spade clanging on to the floor.

"Aagh!" yelled Carl. "Call him off!"

Gary hesitated, looking bewildered, and helpless. Bramble stood watching, but did nothing to help his master.

"Good boy, Tuff," said Neil calmly. He could see that, despite Carl's protests, Tuff had only gripped Carl's sleeve, and hadn't hurt him at all. "Hold on, Tuff."

Tuff didn't need to be told. He had no intention of letting go. Bramble sat up suddenly, and for a moment Neil wondered what he'd do if the dog tried to defend Carl. The stout little black dog was alert and listening, his head tilted to one side. Footsteps could be heard hurrying toward them.

Neil heard Mr. Grey calling his name.

Carl heard the voice, too. With a furious effort he tore free from Tuff and made a dash for the trees, inadvertently rushing headlong into the arms of Mr. Grey and one of his burly farmhands. Tuff darted after him to take hold of his prisoner again. Chris appeared, looking around anxiously for Neil. Sam barked beside him.

Gary looked from Tuff to Carl, then from Neil to the farmer and from Mr. Grey to Bramble on the floor. He was pathetic in defeat. He resigned himself to the hopelessness of the situation and didn't even bother to try and stand up again.

A screech of cars came from the road on the other side of the trees, and two police officers rushed in and grabbed the poachers.

Another dog's bark joined in the noise and Sam rushed out of the trees and ran to Neil's side.

"Sam!" called Neil with relief. The dog jumped up at him and, for once, Neil didn't mind Sam's enthusiastic pawing on his T-shirt. Tuff scampered up to Sam and enjoyed an equally warm welcome.

Chris slapped Neil on the back with equal energy. "Tuff was awesome, wasn't he? I saw his attack on the poacher just as we arrived."

"You cut it close, buddy," Neil panted. "But I'm glad you're here."

The two friends stood and watched the officers lead the two brothers to one of the cars in the road. Mr. Grey began showing another officer some of the stolen items in the old icehouse. He turned and found the boys staring at him. He gave them a thumbs-up sign and smiled.

Neil and Chris suddenly felt very grateful that it was all over.

On a warm evening at Priorsfield Farm, a week later, Neil, Emily, and Sarah were all enjoying a special occasion. They were sitting at the edge of some trees, well back from the riverbank, keeping perfectly still. Their eyes were fixed on a stretch of water by the willow tree, watching a family of otters playing in the river. The otter cubs Neil and Chris had discovered on their previous visit had grown more confident, teasing one another and play-fighting as they tumbled in and out of the water. Their mother, graceful and alert, glided around them. The remains of a small fish she had caught for them lay across the nearby tree roots.

"This is great," Emily said softly. "I've never seen anything like this. They're beautiful." Emily was lying flat on her stomach, her camera poised to take a picture of the enchanting scene before them. "Look at the littlest one. He's floating on his back. Look at his tiny paws!"

"That one's me," said Sarah, "and the biggest one is Neil, and the one wriggling around is Emily."

Emily clicked the shutter and her camera whirred as the film advanced. "I'm glad you found the poachers when you did, Neil. The idea of these sweet otters being taken away to be playthings or a fur coat is terrible. What will happen to the poachers?"

"Dad says they'll be appearing in court soon," replied Neil, keeping his eyes on the water. "Most likely, they'll be fined and their gear confiscated."

"Including Bramble?"

"Including Bramble, yes," said Neil. "But don't worry, Mom said she thinks Dad has got a lead on a good home for him. I'm not sure of the details yet. The poachers will be put under some sort of supervision order. Someone will keep an eye on them and make sure they behave themselves. I felt sorry for Gary. He didn't have much of a clue what he was doing. He thought his brother was wonderful, so he did everything he was told."

They laughed as a tangle of playful otter cubs rose to the surface. After an hour, and as they began to feel the evening grow cooler, Neil, Emily, and Sarah slipped away as quietly as they could.

Harry Grey and Bob Parker came striding out to meet them as they came within sight of the farmyard. Tuff bounded happily up to them, greeted everyone with excited leaps and barks, then dashed away as if he had important work to do and couldn't stay long. Cap and Mick, without his bandage but still limping, followed more slowly.

"Mick seems a lot better, Mr. Grey. And Cap is still getting around OK, too. You are going to keep her, aren't you?"

The farmer chuckled. "'Course we are. I couldn't let her leave this place. She'll be OK as long as we keep using the whistle you gave me." He patted the device, which he kept on a string around his neck.

"That's great news, Mr. Grey. But what's Tuff in such a hurry about?" asked Neil, and he gave his father a puzzled look across the farmyard.

"I've got a new dog, Neil," said Mr. Grey. "Your father's found a perfect little rescue dog for me, and he's getting along great with Tuff."

"That's great! Is that why Dad's here? Which dog was it? I didn't know we had a suitable dog for you."

"He's a recent arrival, you could say. They're a first-rate duo already!"

Mr. Grey and Neil looked toward the barn when they heard rustling and scrambling, and the happy panting of dogs behind a pile of straw bales. Then Neil heard a scuffle. There was a flash of movement and an excited little black-and-tan dog dashed out from between the bales with pieces of straw in his coat. He shook himself, sneezed, and tunneled back in again, having the time of his life.

"It's Bramble!" shouted Neil, and his face lit up with joy. "Bramble and Tuff! They're the perfect team!"